# The House At The Bottom Of The Garden

# The House At The Bottom Of The Garden

By

Michael Madden

Illustrated By

Chelsea Buivids

# Other Titles by Michael Madden

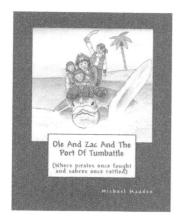

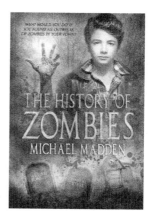

# The House At The Bottom Of The Garden

# Chapter 1

# The House At The Bottom Of The Garden

At the bottom of the garden, if you look closely, you will find a house. It is a very small house, hidden away behind bushes or trees, but it will be there, if you look closely. The house belongs to the Hortibobs, a strange family of creatures that make sure that the garden that they live in is neat, tidy, and full of flowers, fruit and vegetables.

The Hortibobs are secretive, they like to keep themselves hidden, but if you do see one they will be a little bit like a tiny person. They have arms and legs, and they wear clothes made out of leaves, grass and other things that can be found in the garden. Their hands are rough, and they have stubby, strong fingers, useful for gripping. Their feet are covered in hair the colour of straw, and their toes are long and curly. When they are young they have a pale yellow skin, but as they get older they become a yellowish green.

They live with their families, and they have names just like you and I. The family of the Danegolds look after Mrs Smith's garden on the east side of town. It is hard work because Mrs Smith also has a huge vegetable patch and a greenhouse. The Buttergloves live in Mr and Mrs Wilson's garden, which is actually a backyard. Mrs Wilson likes to keep her flowers in pots, and she hates weeds. Fiona Butterglove and her family spend most of their time replacing dandelions after Mrs Wilson pulls them up. Ma and Pa Bluecup live on a farm. They have a very large area to tend to, but their biggest job is trying to stop Nellie the pig and her twelve piglets from eating everything in sight.

# Chapter 2

## The Daffolilys

Our story is about a family of Hortibobs called the Daffolilys, who live in the garden of Mr Johnson. Grandfather Daffolily, also known as "Pops", is one hundred years old. He is short, with grey hair, and unlike the other Daffolilys his face is a deep red through eating too much beetroot juice. Grandmother Daffolily, who answers to the name of "Pips", stays in the house most of the time. She makes all of the Daffolily clothes, and she brews a delicious tea made from nettles and dandelions.

Momma Daffolily does most of the cooking, and the cleaning. She also makes the list of jobs that the family need to do to keep Mr Johnson's garden looking pretty.

Poppa Daffolily does some of the work in the garden, but he spends most of his time hiding away in the garden shed, reading old newspapers, and admiring the growing collection of garden tools that Mr Johnson keeps in there.

When he does come out, Poppa Daffolily can be heard shouting orders to the younger Daffolilys, and muttering to himself that they are not doing the job as well as he would have done it.

There are six Daffolily children, and like all Hortibobs they love to play. Adam, Lucy, Jack and Ruby are all old enough to work in the garden for most of the day, but Phoenix and Miles are still learning about the dangers that can be hiding in the weeds, and they are not allowed out on their own.

Adam is the oldest, the tallest, and the strongest. His muscles bulge out of his shirt, and he does most of the heavy jobs in the garden. Lucy is the oldest girl, but she loves to dress more like her brothers. For gardening work she likes to wear her green leafy jeans and a shirt. She ties her long blonde hair up in a bun that she can tuck beneath her red baseball cap, which is made out of dried beetroot.

Jack and Ruby are twins. They are not identical, but they both have happy round faces and curly ginger hair. Phoenix is small, with brown hair and trendy glasses. Despite her size she is quite strong, and she is probably the smartest of all of the Daffolily children.

Miles has a mop of blonde hair. He is always investigating things and trying to find out how things work. He loves to find toys left out on Mr Johnson's lawn, quite often hiding them so that he can play with them and take them apart later.

# The Daffolily Family Tree

Momma Danegold

Poppa Danegold

Momma Daffolily

Poppa Daffolily

Pips

Pops

Adam

Jack

Lucy

Miles

Ruby

Phoenix

Their house is small, but inside it never seems like that. The walls are made from stones and mud, and the doors and windows are built from sticks and twigs. On top of the house, the roof is mainly old tree roots, though sometimes it is coated in leaves to keep the rain out. A chimney reaches up into the sky, and they like nothing more than a roaring fire in the winter.

However, our story begins in the spring.

# Chapter 3

## Spring

It was early morning when they heard Momma Daffolily singing in the kitchen. The children made their weary way downstairs, wondering what made their mother so happy.

"It's spring," said Momma Daffolily, breaking into another song.

"How do you know?" asked Phoenix, wiping the sleep out of her eyes.

"Oh, you just know," said her mother. "When you are as old as Poppa and me you just know, and today is most definitely spring. Listen."

The kitchen fell quiet, but outside they could hear birds singing. Momma Daffolily lifted a vase from the edge of the sink and placed it on the kitchen table. The vase was filled with bluebells.

"I picked these this morning," Momma continued. "Now watch."

She took a teaspoon and gently tapped each bluebell.

"Ting, tong, ting-a-ling," the bells made tiny sounds that were hard to hear. Momma Daffolily tapped them again, and this time the sound of the bluebells was louder.

"There," she said. "Bluebells don't make a sound until spring, so it is most definitely spring. Now, get your breakfast, we have a lot to do."

Miles groaned as he poured himself some dandelion squash, but Momma Daffolily was already prepared.

"Phoenix and Miles, you can cover the grass with morning dew. Lucy, you can keep an eye on them. Adam, you can deal with the weeds, and Ruby you can break open the bulbs. They will be expecting crocuses and tulips before too long. Jack, you can check the seeds."

The children sat there, nibbling on toast and berries and sipping juice oh so slowly to put off the day's work.

"Come on," said Momma Daffolily, clapping her hands. "The garden won't look after itself, now off you go."

Lucy took Phoenix and Miles to a large tub. The tub had a sign on it that read *Morning Dew*. She gave them a small water pistol each, and told them to march up and down, spraying every inch of the lawn. Miles quickly filled his pistol, pointed it at Phoenix and squirted. Phoenix closed her eyes tightly and squealed as Miles laughed. She was now quite wet, but she filled her own pistol and soaked Miles.

"Stop it!" Lucy said, stamping her feet.

Miles and Phoenix immediately stopped, but Miles could not help himself from giggling.

"There is a lot of lawn and you need to cover it all before any of the Johnsons wake up. Now get on with it."

They sprayed and sprayed, and more went on themselves than on the grass, but after a while the sunlight glistened on every drop of dew.

"Very good," said Lucy. The young Daffolilys both smiled. "Now all you have to remember is to do it every morning until the end of summer." She laughed as their smiles turned to groans.

"Come on, let's go and help Ruby," and Lucy led them to the flower bed where Ruby was surrounded by flower bulbs.

Ruby's little fingers were covered in dirt. She had to dig up the bulbs, open them up so that the flowers could grow, and bury them again. Her head drooped with exhaustion, and Lucy, Miles and Phoenix sat beside her to help.

Miles dug into the soil and pulled out a crocus bulb. It was tightly wrapped and looked as though nothing could grow from it. He

scraped and scratched but the bulb held firm.
Lucy took the bulb and she tried to open it.

Phoenix stood up and looked around. She
picked up a sharp twig and then she took the
bulb from Lucy. The pale brown bulb was
shiny and smooth, with no way of breaking it

open, but Phoenix held it tightly. She poked the twig into the gap at the top, and she twisted. At first there was no movement, but then the outside layers of the bulb split open to reveal a small green shoot that would eventually become a crocus.

"Its just like peeling an onion," she said, and she dug into the soil for another bulb.

Ruby smiled with a fresh burst of energy. Lucy found three more twigs, and the four children quickly finished off the tough job of opening all of the bulbs.

On the other side of the garden, Jack was also covered in soil, but his wide grin told the others that he was enjoying himself. His job was to dig down into the seed beds and make sure that the seeds were growing the right way up.

There were lots of different kinds of seeds, some big and some small, but every one had to be pointed upwards.

His other job was to make sure that the seeds were far enough apart, and that was more difficult.

"Why does Mr Johnson just throw all of the carrot and lettuce seeds on top of each other?" asked Jack. "There are hundreds of them, and they are all on top of each other."

He put handfuls of seeds from the soil into the sack on his back, and then put them back in the ground, each one a few inches away from the next.

Lucy laughed as Jack rummaged through the soil. He was throwing it everywhere and making sure that all of the children were covered in dirt.

Adam marched over, carrying a basket full of green shoots. "What's all the noise?" he asked. "Come and help to spread these."

"What are those?" asked Phoenix.

"Nettles, thistles, buttercups, dandelions, you know. Everything that the garden needs. Mr Johnson calls them *weeds*, but some are much prettier than his other flowers, and nettle tea is delicious."

They each took a handful of weeds and planted them around the borders, on the lawn, in the vegetable patch, and anywhere that was spare ground. When it was all done, they made their way back inside, where Momma Daffolily was waiting to greet them.

"Well done children, and especially Phoenix for finding a quick way to open the bulbs. Now, spring is a very busy time, and we have to keep doing all of those jobs every day."

"Oh no. How long for?" asked Miles.

"Until the summer comes, of course," said Momma Daffolily. "Then we move on to the summer jobs."

# Chapter 4

## Summer

One fine summer morning Momma Daffolily had almost completed her list of jobs, and she was picking through her vegetables, deciding what to put in the composter, and what to put in the pot for dinner. Poppa Daffolily had already been out in the garden for more than an hour, and he burst into the kitchen, grumbling under his breath.

"Hrrmph, hrrmph, Adam and Lucy," he said, pulling out a chair so that he could sit at the table. "Hrmmph, daisies and dandelions. Daisies and dandelions."

"Stop your moaning, its too early for a break," said Momma Daffolily, throwing an onion into her enormous cooking pot.

"Those children," Poppa Daffolily continued. "Can't even pull up a daisy."

Out in the garden, Adam was scratching his head. Mr Johnson had mowed the lawn the previous day, and now Adam and Lucy had to replace all of the daisies and dandelions, to make it look pretty again.

"I don't know why Mr Johnson isn't more careful," said Adam. "Every time he cuts the grass he chops all of the daisies into little pieces. Dandelions too. And clover. It can take us *hours* to put it right."

"Well you better get on with it then," said Phoenix, ruffling her brother's hair as she ran past. Phoenix's job was quite simple. She and Miles had to cover the whole garden in morning dew as they had been doing every day since the spring. That is apart from the occasional days when they forgot, and Mr

Johnson would find his garden rather dry first thing in the morning.

Adam stamped his foot on the ground and listened for a response. None came so he tried it again, and this time the earth moved ever so slightly just in front of him.

Below ground Lucy was in one of the many tunnels that criss-crossed the garden. The tunnels allowed the Daffolilys to move about unseen, even in the daytime. It was also how they pushed up flowers and plants from underground whenever it was time for them to grow. Lucy had a bunch of daisies in her basket, as well as plenty of buttercups and two dandelions. She was working with Adam to replace those that had been chopped up by the lawnmower.

Holding a daisy firmly in her hand, she pushed it through the ceiling of the tunnel. As she pushed, the petals eventually broke through the grass, often covering her in a shower of soil. Adam pulled, Lucy pushed, and sometimes they hit a blockage or a stone, which meant that Lucy pulled and Adam pushed.

Eventually all of the flowers were replaced, and Mr Johnson's neatly mown lawn was once again decorated with colourful flowers. Mr Johnson did not seem to appreciate all of the work that went into this, and he would moan and stomp about.

Lucy appeared next to three daisies that she had just pushed up into the light. Miles was on the other side of the daisies, holding his bucket that was filled with the water that he was spraying. Lucy surprised him, and the bucket tipped. He tried to steady it, but it had a mind of his own. The water slopped and the bucket overturned.

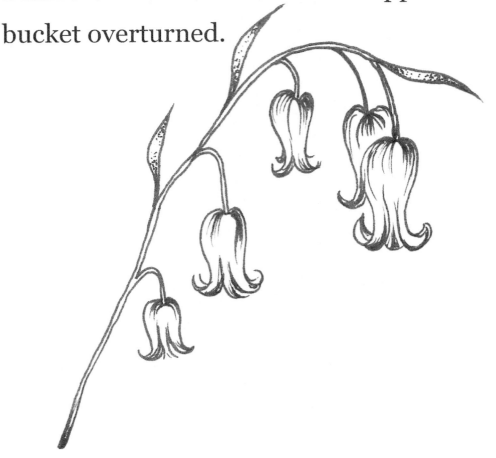

Lucy swirled around at the same moment, and the water gushed out. It knocked her over, and soaked her work clothes, her face and her hair. She got up and chased after Miles, but only in a playful way. The shower was actually quite refreshing after the heat of the tunnels.

The next morning Mr Johnson spent a long time in his greenhouse. Poppa Daffolily huffed and puffed as he waited for Mr Johnson to finish whatever he was doing.

"Hrrmph," he said. "Hrrmph, hrrmph, hrrmph. Must get on, hrrmph. Things to do, hrrmph."

"What things?" said Momma Daffolily. She was quite used to Poppa Daffolily mumbling and grumbling without much cause. "The *only* thing you need to do is to polish the tomatoes for the show."

She paused, but Poppa Daffolily did not respond.

"Mr Johnson might be polishing them himself," she said, laughing out loud.

Poppa Daffolily frowned. "HRRMPH," he said. "Do them himself? He wouldn't know where to start. That's why he only won third in show last year."

The door to the greenhouse opened, and Mr Johnson emerged carrying a tray of plants. Poppa Daffolily strained his eyes to see what they were, and he groaned.

"Oh no, best tell the children," he said. "He's got runner beans, peas, and if I'm not mistaken, sweet peas too. It will take all day to deal with those."

Mr Johnson went to his vegetable patch and planted his runner beans amongst the bamboo canes. Next, he put sticks into the ground in front of the Sunny Wall, and planted his peas. The Daffolilys called it the Sunny Wall because it seemed to soak up the sun all day long. Although the beans and peas were only young plants, they were large enough for the soil, and they had the tell-tale tendrils sprouting from them.

Momma Daffolily summoned Adam, Lucy, Jack, Ruby, Miles and Phoenix. As they gathered in the kitchen, Poppa Daffolily searched through the cupboards, eventually holding up a pale yellow cloth and a spray bottle in triumph.

"We have a very busy day today children," said Momma Daffolily.

"You do," said Poppa Daffolily, "and so do I." Waving his cloth in the air he headed for the door. He paused, looked over his shoulder and said, "Don't miss any!" before walking out into the sunshine.

"Don't miss any what?" asked Miles.

"Well," said Momma Daffolily. "Mr Johnson has just planted out his runner beans and peas. That means we have to make sure they grow up the canes and sticks. Like this."

She reached across to the windowsill and grabbed a plant pot. The pot held a pea plant that was already bursting with green growth. She put the pot onto the table, and the Daffolily children huddled closer to look at it.

"This is a pea," said Momma Daffolily. "You will see the leaves," and she stroked the flimsy green leaves, before reaching for the thin, wiry growths, "and the fingers. You must wrap each finger around the sticks so that they don't flop onto the soil, and instead reach for the sky."

"I can reach for the sky," said Phoenix, thrusting her arms upwards.

"And that's exactly what peas must do," said Momma Daffolily. "You can do the same with the runner beans. Now off you go."

The six Daffolily children marched out of the house, their footsteps echoing off the stone floor. Mr Johnson was nowhere to be seen, and so they headed for the vegetable patch.

Meanwhile, Poppa Daffolily was in the greenhouse. He looked along the neat rows of plants, some in pots, some in trays. There were flowers, vegetables, and some that he was unsure of. At the far end, safely away from all of the other plants, there were four black pots. Inside the pots there were green, ornamental leaves, and fruit in various stages of ripening. These were unmistakeably tomatoes. On two of the plants the tomatoes were green turning to orange, but on the other two they were a bright and shiny red.

On the wall behind the tomatoes there was a rosette. Its blue ribbons were fading, but it was still possible to read *3ʳᵈ place* in the centre.

Poppa Daffolily glanced up at it. "Hrrmph. Third. Won't do. Just won't do. Should be getting first place."

He clambered up onto the shelf and studied the red tomatoes.

"Nice shape," he said out loud. It was almost as if he was the judge. "Good colour, needs a polish."

He pressed the nearest tomato with his finger. The red skin was smooth, and he smiled.

"Plump but firm, just as it should be," he said, and he took his water bottle and cloth from his pocket.

The water bottle let out a fine spray that dusted the tomatoes, and when he rubbed them with his cloth they shone like the sun. He peered into one of them, then sprayed more water, and scrubbed with his cloth again.

Poppa Daffolily spent around five minutes repeating the process, and when he was finished he was pleased that he could almost see his own reflection in the skin of the bright red tomato.

Outside in the garden, Phoenix was very good at twisting the tendrils so that the beans could climb up to the sky. Her small hands and nimble fingers were made for the job. Lucy and Adam helped her to reach the higher places, as Ruby, Jack and Miles tended to the peas.

Phoenix had just about finished, but as she turned she realised that she was quite high up, and between her and the ground was a huge monster. A caterpillar had crawled on to the base of a bean plant, and was now making its way towards her. Of course, the caterpillar was not really huge, but to a Hortibob it was as big as a bear.

She screamed, and Adam laughed. He had seen many caterpillars, and he was not scared of them. Adam knew exactly what to do. He jumped up alongside the caterpillar, and the insect turned to look at him. As it stared, he reached under its chin and tickled it. The caterpillar shuddered. Its pale green body rippled, and it lost its grip. As it fell to the ground, Phoenix clambered down the beanstalk and ran to where Ruby and Miles were still stretching out the tendrils.

"That's enough beans for me today," she said, and she set off back towards the house.

The rest of the family followed, laughing at the caterpillar incident. Phoenix felt silly, now that she knew that the way to deal with a caterpillar was to tickle it under its chin.

The following day Poppa Daffolily was woken by some banging and thumping, and the whole house shook. As he peered through the window he was dismayed to see Mr Johnson's grandson playing football in the garden.

"Oh no," he said to himself. "The grass will be ruined."

He went into the kitchen, where Momma Daffolily had already made breakfast which consisted of dandelion pancakes with fresh raspberries. She had also laid out three pots of paint that were all labelled *Green Grass*.

Poppa Daffolily groaned. "I hope he doesn't do too much damage. That paint gets everywhere."

"Now, now, Poppa," said Momma Daffolily. "The children can help. It will be done in no time."

"The children can help with what?" asked Adam, as he sat down and helped himself to the biggest pancake.

"There are children playing football on the lawn, so we have to fix the grass when they have finished. You can take Miles and Jack to paint the grass so that it is a healthy green again, whilst Lucy and Phoenix can do the roses."

"Do the roses?" asked Phoenix.

"Yes. Its getting to the middle of summer, and we need the roses to smell nice." She reached up to a high shelf and brought down three glass bottles. "You can spray them with this perfume."

A short time later, when they were sure that the football game had finished, Miles, Adam and Jack took a pot of paint each and went out onto the lawn. There were bare

patches, and some of the grass had become dirty. They splashed paint where it was needed, and soon had the lawn looking bright and green. Unfortunately, Miles was not used to painting, and he was looking bright and green too, as most of his pot of paint had splashed onto his hands, face and clothes.

"There's only one thing for it," said Poppa Daffolily, "and that's the hose."

Miles had to stand with his arms and legs out, as Poppa Daffolily sprayed him with a hose to wash off the green paint whilst it was still wet. Miles squealed at first, but then he began to enjoy it, as it was already becoming a rather warm day.

Meanwhile, Lucy and Phoenix crossed the garden, edging past where their brothers were painting, and came to a flower bed that contained twenty or more roses. Some were red, some were yellow, but most of them were white.

"We have to be careful," said Lucy, "because roses have thorns, and thorns can hurt!"

Phoenix was too impatient. She grabbed the first bottle and was about to spray the perfume when Lucy stopped her. "Wait," she said. "You have to match the colour to the right bottle."

Phoenix looked at the bottle in her hand which had a label on it that said *Red*. She looked up to see that she was standing beneath a yellow rose. "Oh no," she thought. "That's not right."

She picked up a different bottle and this time it said *Yellow*, so she started to spray the bright yellow petals. A lot of the spray missed and came back down, covering Phoenix and Lucy with the beautiful perfume.

They laughed, and used up the full bottle of yellow perfume, before moving on to the red, and finally the white. When they were done the whole garden smelt of roses, which was not a bad thing, but Momma Daffolily was cross that she would now have to fill her bottles with more perfume.

The vegetable patch was a place for hard work, but it could have its rewards. One morning Adam and Lucy were busy underground stretching the carrots.

The problem with carrots is that they can become twisty and not straight at all, so the Hortibobs burrow beneath them, remove all of the stones, and then pull the carrots by their beards to make them long and straight. It is a job that nobody likes. When they had finished, Adam's wiry brown hair was full of dark, black soil, and Lucy's blue pinafore dress was covered in mud and hair from the carrots.

It would be a while before Phoenix would be strong enough to fix the carrots, but she watched Adam and Lucy, fascinated at how the carrots stretched. She did not know that carrots actually have beards!

Next to the carrots was a patch of potatoes. Potatoes out of the ground were a great favourite with Mr Johnson, but they were also very popular with the Hortibobs. Adam burrowed from the carrots and soon found himself surrounded by juicy potatoes, each one as big as his head. He scrambled upwards, and as he broke the surface Lucy collected the potato that he had pulled from the ground. He went back into the soil, and soon Lucy gathered a second potato, and then a third.

Lucy and Adam lay back under the shade of some lettuce leaves, and munched on the raw potatoes. Phoenix nuzzled in between them, and for the first time she tasted the earthy but sweet crunch of a new potato.

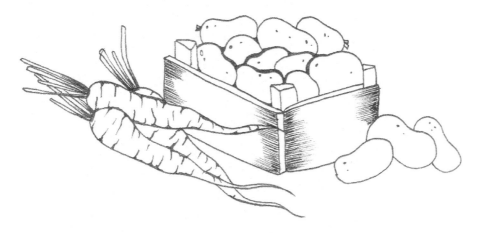

*Chomp, chomp* was the only sound that could be heard for a while, until Momma Daffolily called out to them that it was dinner time. She was surprised to find that they were not very hungry.

One day, as the summer drew to a close, Mr Johnson came into the garden with a beaming smile across his face. It was the day that Poppa Daffolily had been waiting for. Mr Johnson went into the greenhouse, where he seemed to stay for an age. Poppa Daffolily waited impatiently for him to leave, stomping up and down, and leaning forward to see what he could see.

Eventually Mr Johnson opened the door and left the greenhouse. He walked down to the bottom of the garden, carrying a garden fork. This was Poppa Daffolily's chance. He rushed through the open door and climbed on to the shelf.

There it was. A giant red rosette with the words *Tomato* and *Best In Show* and *First* written in large black letters.

All of his hard work had paid off, and Poppa Daffolily returned to his kitchen. He did not have to tell Momma Daffolily the good news, she could tell just by looking at his face.

At the bottom of the garden, Mr Johnson stuck his garden fork into the ground, ready to dig up the potato crop. To his disappointment there were only a handful of potatoes.

"I wonder why there are so few potatoes?" he said out loud. "I have done everything right. The soil, the watering, everything. It's a complete mystery."

He carried on digging but found nothing, except for one or two very small potatoes that had tiny teeth marks in them.

# Chapter 5

## Autumn

One particular morning Lucy woke up shivering. It was colder than the day before, and the sky was grey with rain clouds. She looked out of the window, staring at the gloom, hoping for something to brighten the day.

Suddenly, there it was. Floating this way and that, gliding on the breeze, and flipping over as it was caught by a gust of wind. It was flat and brown, and closer inspection showed that it was a leaf from an oak tree. As it landed on the ground, Lucy looked up. Another leaf appeared, and then another. Soon the sky was filled with falling leaves.

"*This can only mean one thing,*" she thought, and she leapt out of bed.

"Its autumn," she cried at the top of her voice, and she danced with joy down the stairs and into the kitchen.

Autumn is a fun time for Hortibobs, and the jobs seem to be a lot easier than the hard work of spring and summer.

"Breakfast is almost..." Momma Daffolily's words faded as Lucy rushed past her and into the garden.

The lawn was covered with a brown carpet of leaves. As each puff of wind blew, more leaves fell onto the grass, the vegetable patch, and the flower beds. Lucy gathered huge handfuls and threw them up into the air. She loved the crunching sound that they made, she loved their gentle touch as they brushed her hands and face on their way back down to the ground, and she loved their smell. It was the smell of, well, of leaves!

She went back inside where Phoenix and Miles were already dressed and eating raspberry pancakes.

"Hurry up," she said. Her red face was filled with excitement.

"Not so fast," said Poppa Daffolily. "There are lots of jobs to do before you have your fun. Now get some breakfast. We have a long day ahead."

Adam was next to appear, and he was dressed in a heavy coat with large boots. Thick gloves covered his hands.

"I'm off to see to the brambles," he said. "Anyone coming?"

"Me," said Phoenix, and her hand shot up into the air.

Phoenix thought that the bramble patch was a perfect place to start the day, with all of that delicious fruit, but Adam had a different plan. He threw some gloves to Phoenix.

"Put those on and come on," he said, already half way out of the door.

Phoenix followed him past the vegetable patch, where the green beans were swollen and ready to pick, and on to the rough part of the garden that no one really looked after. Here, there were wild blackberries and raspberries, poking in and out of the fence.

They had picked and eaten lots of these over the past few weeks, and Momma had made delicious jams, pies and pancakes. Mr Johnson did not seem to bother with this wild fruit, but the Hortibobs knew how good it was.

Poppa Daffolily arrived, covered from head to toe in a suit that was made out of bark, and not even his hands could be seen.

"Now young Phoenix," he said, bending down which made his wooden suit rattle, "if the brambles stay under control at the bottom of the garden, Mr Johnson will leave them alone, but if they get out of hand and spread into his vegetable patch, he might be tempted to dig them up. No more blackberry pancakes, and no more raspberry jam!"

Phoenix's mouth dropped open. "No more raspberry jam? What will we do?"

"We won't let it happen," said Adam, standing in front of a particularly prickly blackberry bush. "These brambles need to be twisted back behind the fence."

He pulled out a sharp knife made of stone. "If you see any long ones, I will cut them back, but mostly we just want to twist them back behind the fence."

They got to work, and Phoenix struggled to get the hang of it. She pulled on a bramble, but as she was about to thread it back through the fence, it slipped from her grasp and sprang back to where it was before. She grabbed it with both hands and pulled it hard. With a huge effort she turned and twisted, poking it through a hole in the wire fence. She twisted it again, let go, and this time the bramble stayed in place, tucked neatly away. However, she realised that she had trapped herself between the fence and the bramble. She was stuck!

"Help," she cried. "Help!"

Adam quickly snipped both ends of the bramble and Phoenix was free.

"Go and help with the kins," he said pointing to the large, leafy plants that were in the vegetable patch.

"Kins?" said Phoenix. "What are kins?"

"Pumpkins, of course," laughed Poppa Daffolily. "They used to be small, about the size of a tomato, and they were called kins. Now we have to pump them up to their giant orange size, and so we call them pumpkins."

Phoenix walked across to the vegetable patch, where Miles was measuring the size of a bright orange pumpkin with his outstretched arms. Jack was using bellows to pump up the pumpkin, and Ruby was ready with the grey stopper that would prevent the air from escaping. The pumpkin swelled.

"Bit more," said Miles, and Jack pumped.

"Bit more," said Miles, and Jack pumped again.

"Bit m..." but Miles did not finish.

A loud "pop" was followed by a burst of orange and yellow mush. The pumpkin had exploded, and Phoenix, Jack, Ruby and Miles were all covered in pumpkin. They laughed, but realised that they might get into trouble, so they quickly moved on to the next pumpkin.

After a while the pumpkins were all lined up in neat rows, all except the one that had exploded. Poppa Daffolily looked at them, but before he could ask about the patch of mush Jack called him away. "Come on, we need to do the acorns, and conkers, and helicopters."

"No so fast," said Poppa Daffolily. "Mushrooms and toadstools first."

He produced a large sack and emptied it out onto the lawn. "Now," he continued, "these need to be placed under the trees. Be careful with the red ones, they are poisonous. Give you a nasty rash, and worse."

Phoenix picked up three white mushrooms. They were quite small with long, thin stalks. She carefully scraped away some earth and planted them. Their white caps pointed proudly up at the sky, and she went back to the pile. There were brown ones, flat ones, purple ones and fluffy ones, and she was happy to pick up any of those. However, the red ones that Poppa had warned her about looked scary. They had a pointed tip, and their red caps were covered in large white spots. Their fat stems were like swollen legs, and they gave off a strong, rotten smell.

Fortunately Adam planted all of the red ones, and the job was soon complete.

"Well done," said Poppa, grinning with pride and gathering up his sack. "Now you can deal with the acorns and whatnots."

Mr Johnson's garden was surrounded by large trees. There was a huge, old oak, a horse chestnut, and a sycamore. All of the Daffolilys, including Poppa, loved the next part of their autumn chores.

They began with the oak, clambering up the highest branches, then locating the acorns. With a quick twist they threw them to the ground, taking care not to hit the pair of squirrels who gathered as many of the fallen acorns as they could to prepare for the winter. At the same time they shook the branches. More and more leaves tumbled and swayed to the ground, creating large, soft piles. They moved to the middle branches and did the same, then the lower branches. Once they were all finished they jumped into the leafy mounds. It was quite a long way for a Daffolily to jump, but the leaves gave them a soft landing.

Of course, the younger Daffolilys could not just land on the leaves, they had to roll about and throw some at their brothers and sisters. It was a fun time, but Poppa reminded them that there was still work to do.

Next it was the horse chestnut. Once again they climbed to the very top, but this time the job was a little more tricky. They had to prize apart each stiff and prickly green globe to reveal the brown conker inside. Sometimes they threw the whole thing down, hoping to break open the conker as it fell, but then they had to be careful not to land on them when they jumped, as that would be painful.

Finally, it was the sycamore. The sycamore had *helicopters* for seeds. These were like wings, and if they found two stuck together they could have great fun. Adam did find two together and he saved them until last. Phoenix and Miles also found a pair, and finally Jack. Ruby and Lucy did not care for the helicopters, and Poppa was probably a little too old.

So, Adam, Phoenix, Miles and Jack plucked their helicopters from the branch. They held them out and leapt into the air. The helicopters spun as they fluttered to the ground, and each Daffolily spun with them. It was a long way down, and by the time they reached the ground they were all quite dizzy.

Miles tried to get up but his feet were out of control. Phoenix lay down and looked at the sky which was spinning fast above her. Adam, who had done this many times before, closed his eyes tightly, shook his head, and the dizziness soon disappeared. Jack was learning, and he followed his older brother's example.

Miles and Phoenix clambered up to the lower branches again. They found more helicopters and squealed with delight as they fluttered down again, ignoring the dizziness that they felt.

The piles of leaves were now as tall as Adam, but they could not simply be left as they were. The Daffolilys final job for the day was to spread them far and wide. The dry leaves crunched and swooshed as they gathered them up and scattered them into the air, and of course they would often throw them at each other, just for fun.

Mr Johnson would have a huge job on his hands scooping up all of these fallen leaves, but that was no concern of the Daffolilys. They were preparing themselves for the cold days of winter.

# Chapter 6

## Winter

"Is that snow?" asked Momma Daffolily, standing in the doorway. She held out her hand, expecting a snowflake to fall on it.

After a few seconds the first snowflake landed, gently melting with the warmth of her palm. Then another fell, and another. Soon her hand was covered, and she quickly went inside.

"Boots and fur today," she said, "it's winter!"

Through the window she could see Poppa Daffolily stomping about next to the vegetable patch. Poppa was keen to get the whole of the garden tidy and ready for winter, but he had found an area that was going to take a lot of work.

"Mud!" he said. "Thick, grey, mud. Nothing I can do with that. Its just a waste of ground."

He stomped some more and his boots became muddier and muddier. Eventually, one of them was so covered in mud that it became stuck, and Poppa Daffolily could not move it. He pulled with all of his strength, then he stumbled backwards and fell over. As he looked down at his feet, he realised that the left foot was still inside its boot, but the right foot was not. That boot was buried deep in the mud.

He got to his feet and leaned over, standing on one leg to keep his right foot from getting covered in mud. Further and further he stretched, until he realised that he had gone too far. He whirled his arms to try to pull himself backwards, but it was too late. He fell face down. Now it wasn't just his foot that was muddy, his whole body, including his face and his hat, were a brown, muddy mess.

He scrambled to his feet and pulled at the boot. It came free, but he fell over again, this time backwards. Now his front *and* his back were muddy. He would have to get washed down before he could do any more jobs.

Momma had watched the whole thing from the kitchen, and she giggled when Poppa rushed past her. He eyed her suspiciously as he dumped his boots in the hallway, and went off to change his clothes.

All of the children wrapped up warm and prepared to venture out into the garden. There was not a lot of work to do in winter, but there were some very important jobs.

Adam led the way, and he marked out a shape in the centre of the lawn. It was about a metre long and half a metre wide, and he stomped all over it.

"What are you doing?" asked Phoenix.

"I'm making sure that some of the grass pokes through the snow. We wouldn't want it all to get covered," Adam explained.

Phoenix joined in the stomping, but she was still not quite sure why. Lucy made another shape by stomping close by, and she peeled back the grass, carrying it off to the house.

"What is *she* doing?" asked Miles.

"I'm making sure there is still some grass growing in the winter. You might think that the grass does not grow in the winter – but it does!" said Lucy. She laid the grass under the shelter at the side of the house. "The problem is, it grows down instead of up! So if we don't get at least some to grow the right way up, the lawn would be a real mess in the spring."

The garden was quickly filling with snow, so Lucy urged Jack, Ruby, Miles and Phoenix to help. Soon they had quite a few pieces of earth and grass safely stored under the shelter.

"Now, hunt around for acorns," said Adam. "When you find them, step on them to break them open."

Phoenix enjoyed this, crunching the acorns under her boots, but she was puzzled.

"Why do we squash the acorns?"

"They will become frozen in the snow, and when they are frozen they won't open, and if they don't open then they cannot grow into oak trees," Adam explained.

So, they all traipsed around the garden, crushing acorns which at least kept their feet warm. Poppa Daffolily, in fresh clothes and clean boots, joined them and dug up a tiny tree. It was only just taller than Phoenix, but he lifted it gently and carefully carried it off to the house. As he went, he threw a small parcel to Adam who caught it and put it into his pocket.

"Right you lot," he said. "Off to the compost bin. Get that compost working."

They gathered armfuls of dead leaves, plants and grass as they made their way to the bottom of the garden. Here, next to the brambles, they found Mr Johnson's huge compost heap. It was already higher than the fence, but they each climbed up and threw their leaves and plants onto the top.

Adam reached into his pocket and pulled out the parcel that Poppa Daffolily had thrown to him.

"What's that?" asked Miles.

Adam put his finger to his lips. "Shhhh. We don't want everyone to know. This is Poppa's magic compost dust."

Miles stared at the parcel, eyes wide in astonishment.

"There's no such thing as magic dust," said Phoenix, hands on hips.

"Of course there is," said Lucy, "you just have to *believe*."

Adam sprinkled the dust, and almost at once the plants and grass and leaves started to wriggle. Phoenix breathed in with a loud "oooh" at what she saw. The greenery turned grey and then brown, before it sank into the compost heap.

"Right, let's go," said Adam. "By spring that will be the finest compost, and it will certainly help the garden to grow."

They went back to the house where Poppa was planting the tiny tree in a bucket of soil.

"Phoenix, hold this steady for me," he said, and Phoenix grabbed the stem of the tree.

Poppa patted down the soil, but Phoenix looked puzzled.

"Why are you doing this now?" she asked. "Nothing will grow in the winter."

"Ah but it will," said Poppa. "This sapling will grow and grow, all through the winter. By the time spring comes around it will be tall enough to plant out in the garden. Mr Johnson will wonder just where a tree came from, especially one of my winter trees. He will scratch his head, look here and there, but he will never know." Poppa bent down close to Phoenix and lowered his voice to a whisper. "It will be our secret."

"Ooh, our secret," said Phoenix, and she smiled from ear to ear.

Momma Daffolily opened the door to their food store. There were berries, mushrooms, tomatoes, potatoes, peas, and a few carrots. She had even managed to save a few ears of corn, and there was a large jar full of hazelnuts.

"Looks like we will have plenty of food to keep us warm through the winter, until spring arrives," she said.

She gave a pleasant sigh as she sank down into her comfortable chair in front of the fire, sipping on a fresh cup of nettle tea.

# About the author

Michael Madden has worked for many years in the IT industry, as a result of which he has been quoted in publications as prestigious as the New York Times. He continues to work around the globe from Sao Paolo to Kiev and all places in between.

He has self-published several books, including *Ole And Zac And The Port Of Tumbattle*, a rhyming picture book. In 2018 he released *The History Of Zombies*, a novel aimed at getting young teens off their electronic devices and into a book.

Michael has also had one book traditionally published, the authorised biography *Mike Sanchez Big Town Playboy*, for which he interviewed such legendary entertainers as Bill Wyman, Andy Fairweather Low, Albert Lee and Peter Richardson. The foreword was kindly provided by Robert Plant.

He is an avid blogger and occasional podcaster. Many of his podcasts are based on Words And Music, his regular slot on various radio stations for which he interviewed Suzi Quatro, Steve Harley, Carol Drinkwater, Wreckless Eric, Limahl, Marty Wilde, Right Said Fred, and many more.

He has also performed as an after-dinner speaker on a number of occasions, as a result of another of his passions, playing amateur cricket.

Originally from Sale in Cheshire, Michael now lives with his wife Sally in the more peaceful surroundings of Whaley Bridge, in the Peak District.

For information please visit

www.michael-madden.co.uk

# About The Illustrator

Chelsea Buivids is a young, self-taught artist from the Peak District. From an early age she has always loved art and being creative, spending many hours painting and drawing.

This passion began at nursery, when she would have a painting to show her parents on a daily basis.

As she developed her art, she experimented with a variety of mediums, until she eventually began to concentrate on acrylics, gouache, oils, watercolours, pencil and fine liner. More recently she has been experimenting with digital art.

In her spare time she paints animals and wildlife on wood slices, and she offers these for sale on her Etsy store, ChelseasArtShed.

She has always had an interest in illustrating a book, and so was thrilled to be able to work on *The House At The Bottom Of The Garden*, a project that she describes as both exciting and fun.

# Creating The Daffolilys

bluebell
hat

jacle
miles

older ones
pointy noses
younger more round?

grand father    daffodilly

Jack

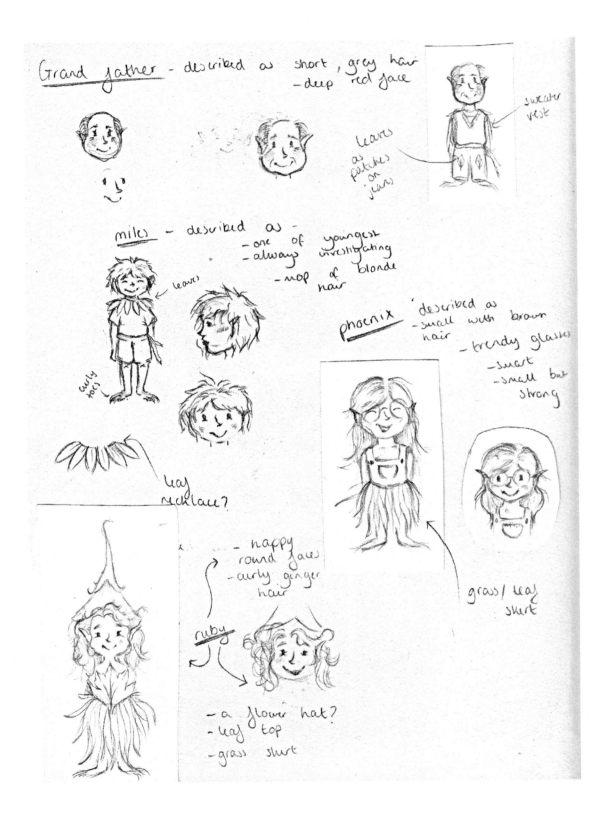

Grandfather - described as short, grey hair
- deep red face

sweater vest

leaves as patches on jeans

miles - described as -
- one of youngest
- always investigating
- mop of blonde hair

leaves

curly toes

leaf necklace?

phoenix described as
- small with brown hair
- trendy glasses
- smart
- small but strong

grass/leaf skirt

- happy round face
- curly ginger hair

ruby

- a flower hat?
- leaf top
- grass skirt

adam → described as    - oldest tallest & strongest
                       - muscles
                       - heavy jobs

does most
heavy jobs
↳ rip in shirt?
neck tie made
with leaves?

grandmother → described as → stays in house most the
                                               time
              - makes most   the clothes

leaf
pocket
on
apron?

lucy - described as → oldest girl
                    → dress like her
                            brothers
                    - green leafy
                      jeans +
                             shirt
                    - long hair
                         in bun
                    - beetroot
                      baseball
                      cap

Jack "happy round
      face - curly
      ginger hair"

dungarees
with leaf
details

beetroot
cap

leafy
jeans

mum — does most cooking + cleaning
(mama daffolily)

leaf earrings

leafy
apron

poppa daffolily — does some work in the garden
— spends most time hiding in garden shed
—